Pony to the Rescue

Do you love ponies? Be a Pony Pal!

Look for these Pony Pal books:

Pony to the Rescue

Jeanne Betancourt

illustrated by Paul Bachem

A
LITTLE APPLE
PAPERBACK

SCHOLASTIC INC.
New York Toronto London Auckland Sydney

ISBN 0-590-25244-5

12 11 10 9 8 7 6 5 4 3 2   5 6 7 8 9/9 0/0

Printed in the U.S.A.   40

First Scholastic printing, July 1995

For my sister, Teri

The author thanks Gay Rickenbacker of Cornerstone Academy and Elvia Gignoux for applying their knowledge of horses to this story.

Contents

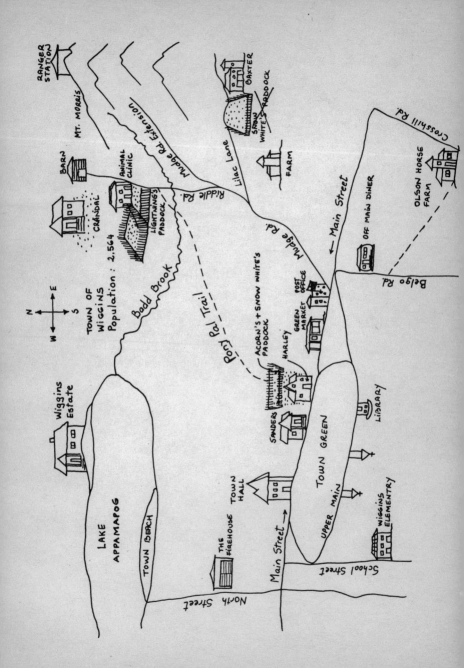

Pony to the Rescue

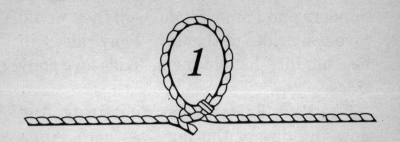

Pony Rides

Anna Harley braided blue ribbons into her pony's black mane. As she worked on Acorn, Anna thought about the day ahead and the annual firehouse fair. She loved the fair the volunteer firemen put on for the people of Wiggins. Every summer Anna went to the fair to play games like ring toss and hit the bottle, eat treats like cotton candy and popcorn, and go on rides like bumper cars and the Ferris wheel.

Anna's father was the volunteer fireman in charge of games and rides. This year her father asked Anna and her friends — Lulu Sanders and Pam Crandal — if they would give pony rides at the fair. "Pony rides will be a big hit," he told them. "Kids love pony rides."

The Pony Pals said yes right away. And now the day of the fair was here. Anna couldn't wait for it to begin!

"How does Snow White look?" Lulu asked Anna.

Anna looked over and saw that Lulu had finished braiding ribbons in her pony's white mane.

"She looks beautiful!" Anna said.

"And Acorn looks so handsome," said Lulu.

"My dad is setting up a rope ring for us," Anna said. "And three of the other firemen are going to help us."

"Help us do what?" asked Lulu.

"They'll walk next to the little kids who are riding," Anna said. "That way we can concentrate on leading the ponies."

"That's a good idea," said Lulu. "There'll

be a lot of kids who've never been on a pony before."

Anna saw Pam Crandal and her pony, Lightning, cantering off Pony Pal Trail. "Here they come," Anna said. Pam lived at the other end of the mile-and-a-half trail that made getting to Anna's house easy.

Pam pulled Lightning up beside the other two ponies. Anna petted Lightning's forehead. "You look great, Lightning!" she said. Pam had braided periwinkle-blue ribbons in Lightning's mane, too. And, like Anna and Lulu, Pam wore her periwinkle-blue vest. They were all wearing the official Pony Pal color for the pony rides.

Anna mounted Acorn and Lulu mounted Snow White. "Let's go to the fair," said Pam.

As the Pony Pals rode up North Street toward the redbrick firehouse, Anna could hear music from the fair rides and the voices of excited children. She even smelled the popcorn and cotton candy.

Lulu pointed ahead. "Look," she said,

"there's already a line of kids waiting for pony rides."

Anna counted five kids in line next to a large painted sign. PONY RIDES $1.00.

When Anna dismounted Acorn, a little girl with straight blonde hair was beside her. "Can I ride that pony? Can I?" she asked.

"Sure," Anna said, "that's what we're here for. His name is Acorn."

The girl rubbed Acorn's neck. "He's so cute," she said. "Acorn, you're the best."

"You'd better go back to the line now," Anna said. "But I'll be sure you get to ride Acorn for your turn."

"Okay," the girl agreed.

"What's your name?" Anna asked.

"Rosalie Lacey," the girl answered as she ran back to her place at the head of the line. "I'm six."

For the next two hours the Pony Pals led their patient ponies around the ring — twice around for each rider.

As Lulu helped a redheaded boy down

from Snow White, she told Anna, "Snow White and Lightning are having a good time. But I think Acorn loves giving pony rides most of all."

Anna agreed. She was proud of her pony. He was gentle with the children and had the cutest expression on his face when they petted him. Anna looked over to see her next rider. It was Rosalie Lacey — again. Acorn noticed Rosalie, too, and neighed softly.

"Are you back for another ride?" Anna asked.

Rosalie handed Anna a ticket. "My mother gave me five dollars for the fair," Rosalie told Anna. "I spent it all on tickets to ride Acorn."

Anna smiled at Rosalie. "Okay," she said. "Let's ride."

As Anna was leading Acorn and Rosalie around the ring, Rosalie asked, "Where does Acorn live? Do you live on a farm or something?"

"We live on Main Street," Anna said.

"Acorn lives in the yard behind my house."

"What house?" Rosalie asked.

"The white one next to the house with the Sanders Beauty Parlor sign," Anna explained.

"I live on School Street!" Rosalie shouted. "That means we're neighbors, Acorn and me. Friends and neighbors." Even though she was in the saddle, Rosalie leaned over and hugged Acorn around the neck.

"Sit up," Anna warned her. "That's not safe."

"Acorn would never hurt me," Rosalie said. "We're best friends."

"He wouldn't hurt you on purpose," Anna explained. "But accidents can happen. If you're going to be around ponies you have to follow some safety rules."

"Can I come visit Acorn?" Rosalie asked. "Please say yes."

"Sure you can," Anna answered. She smiled at the girl. "After all, you're friends and neighbors."

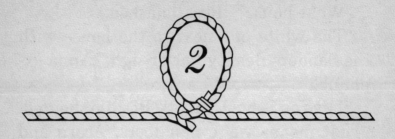

Acorn's New Friend

Later that afternoon, back at the Harley paddock, the Pony Pals cooled down their ponies with wet sponges. Then they scraped off the excess water with sweat scrapers.

"That Rosalie was the cutest kid," Anna told Lulu and Pam. "She's as crazy about ponies as we are."

"She'll be a rider someday for sure," Lulu said.

"She took five pony rides on Acorn," Anna told her friends.

"Kids love Acorn," Pam said. "Look how

my sister and brother always beg to play with him."

Pam Crandal's father was a veterinarian and her mother taught horseback riding. So Pam and the five-year-old Crandal twins — Jack and Jill — grew up around horses and knew a lot about them.

"When I was Rosalie's age," Lulu remembered, "I fell in love with ponies, too. But I didn't get one until I was ten and moved here."

Lulu Sanders moved to Wiggins to stay with her grandmother while her father was working in the Amazon jungle. Now Mr. Sanders was also living at Grandmother Sanders'. Anna knew it made Lulu happy to be with her father again. Lulu's mother died when she was little, so she was especially close to her dad.

"I've had my own pony for as long as I can remember," Pam said.

"She even had one when we were in kindergarten," Anna told Lulu.

"I always gave you turns riding, didn't I?" Pam asked Anna.

"All the time," said Anna. "We had so much fun."

Anna gave her tired pony a handful of oats. "You were terrific today, Acorn," she said. "Thanks."

The next morning, after breakfast and chores, Anna and Lulu saddled up their ponies for a day of trail riding.

Anna heard a girl's voice calling "Acorn! Acorn!" She looked up to see Rosalie Lacey running across the paddock. Rosalie went up to Acorn and gave him a big hug around the neck. Acorn recognized Rosalie and whinnied happily.

"I missed you, too," Rosalie said.

"I guess you found my house," Anna said. She hadn't expected Rosalie to visit so soon.

"Acorn has lived on Main Street all the time and I didn't even know," Rosalie said excitedly.

"Acorn's only been here for a year," Anna told Rosalie. "I got him when I was nine."

"I want a pony, too," Rosalie said. "My mommy won't get me one. She said they're a lot of money. She said we can't even buy a car, why should we have a pony. I told her I liked ponies better than cars."

"Having a pony is a big responsibility," Anna told Rosalie, "and a lot of work."

"I don't care," Rosalie said. She dug her hand into her jean's pocket and pulled out a fistful of coins. "I want another ride on Acorn," she said. "I got money from my piggy bank. See?"

"Pony rides were only for yesterday," Anna told Rosalie.

"We're leaving now anyway," Lulu added. "For a trail ride."

"Can I come?" Rosalie asked. "My mom will let me. All I do all day is go to dumb day camp."

Lulu and Anna exchanged a look. Rosalie was cute, but there was no way they were going to include her on their trail ride.

"We're all experienced riders," Lulu explained. "And besides there are only three ponies."

"I could sit on Acorn with you," Rosalie said to Anna. "I won't wiggle or anything."

"Two in a saddle isn't safe," Anna told her.

Anna checked her saddlebag to be sure she'd packed water with her lunch. Then she swung herself up on Acorn's back.

"We could take turns on Acorn," Rosalie said. "And you can have the most turns. Cross my heart."

Anna shook her head no.

"Pam and Lightning are waiting for us on the trail," Lulu told Rosalie. "We have to go."

"I'll bet you'll do something special today at day camp," Anna said. "Something that's loads of fun."

"I want to play with Acorn today," Rosalie said sadly.

Lulu and Snow White were already going through the open paddock gate.

Rosalie walked alongside Acorn and Anna. "Please let me come," she whined, "please . . ."

Anna moved Acorn into a trot. Rosalie picked up her pace, too. Why couldn't the girl just go to day camp and leave her alone?

"Don't get so close to a moving horse and rider," she warned Rosalie. "You could get hurt."

Rosalie finally gave up and slowed down. Anna and Acorn passed through the paddock gate onto the trail. Anna signaled Acorn to move into a canter. But Acorn slowed to a walk instead.

"What's wrong, Acorn?" Anna asked. Acorn turned his head. He wanted to go back to the paddock. Anna looked behind her.

Rosalie was standing at the gate, looking sad. Acorn turned his head and neighed at the little girl.

Lulu, who was ahead of Anna and Acorn

on the trail, called to Anna, "What's wrong?"

"You go ahead," Anna called back. "We'll catch up." She turned Acorn around. She didn't have to urge her pony to move now. He trotted straight back to the paddock and up to Rosalie.

"Oh, Acorn," Rosalie said. "You came back."

"He's still going on a trail ride," Anna told Rosalie. "But we'll be home around four o'clock. If your mother says it's okay, come over after day camp. You can help me groom and feed him."

"Yippee!" Rosalie cheered. "Did you hear that, Acorn? I'm going to feed you!"

Rosalie's Surprise

Pam and Lulu were waiting for Anna at the three birch trees that marked the midpoint of Pony Pal Trail.

"We thought Rosalie would be riding Acorn and you'd be running along behind them," Lulu joked.

"That girl is crazy about Acorn," Anna said as she leaned over and patted Acorn on the neck. "I can understand why. Acorn's great."

"Are you and your great pony ready to go trail riding?" Pam asked.

"Let's go," Anna answered. It was her turn to lead. She steered Acorn toward the trail on the Wiggins estate that started behind the birch trees. He responded immediately to her direction. He was still her pony.

First the Pony Pals went to their favorite field on the Wiggins estate and took turns jumping their ponies over a low stone wall. Then the ponies munched on fresh grass while the girls ate their lunch beside Badd Brook.

On the way home they stopped by the paddock at Ms. Wiggins' mansion to say hi to her black horse, Picasso, and her old Shetland pony, Winston.

Ms. Wiggins waved to them from her painting studio. They waved back. They all liked Ms. Wiggins. Especially Anna. Anna and Ms. Wiggins had a lot in common. They were both dyslexic and had trouble learning how to read. And they were both terrific artists.

By four o'clock the three girls were back

on Pony Pal Trail. That's when Pam reminded Lulu and Anna that they were going back to her house for a picnic and barn sleepover.

"Oh, no!" Anna said. "I thought that was tomorrow. I told Rosalie she could help me feed and groom Acorn when I got back."

"Maybe she forgot about it," Pam said.

"Are you kidding?" Anna and Lulu said together.

"You could call your house and have your mother tell her to come back tomorrow," Lulu suggested.

"My mother's not home," Anna said. "She's working at the diner. Besides, Rosalie would be so disappointed." Anna sighed. "I gotta go back."

Anna left her friends and galloped home along Pony Pal Trail.

She wasn't at all surprised to find Rosalie waiting for her and Acorn at the paddock gate. Anna slowed the pony down and halted next to Rosalie.

"I have a big surprise for you," Rosalie told Acorn. "Wait till you see."

"And I have a surprise for you," Anna told Rosalie. "How would you like to ride Acorn back to his shelter?"

"Yippee!" Rosalie shouted. She wanted to hold the reins herself, but Anna knew that it was safer if *she* led the pony. "You can get down by yourself," Anna told her.

Anna saw Rosalie's "surprise" before they reached the shelter. It was three *huge* piles of hay laid out on the shelter floor. Each was topped with a mound of oats and carrots.

"I made supper for the ponies," Rosalie bragged. "Where're the other ones?"

Anna tried to stay calm as she explained to Rosalie that the other two ponies were eating at the Crandals'.

"Can Acorn eat his?" Rosalie asked.

"You never give a horse that much food, Rosalie," Anna scolded. "You only give them the exact amount you want them to eat. Overeating can make horses sick. It can even kill them."

"I'll clean it up," Rosalie said quietly.

"I'll do it," Anna told her.

Anna took off Acorn's bridle and saddle. She let Rosalie help her sponge down Acorn and showed her how to use the sweat scraper. Then Anna turned Acorn out in the paddock.

"Can I play with him?" Rosalie asked.

"Yes," Anna said. "But keep him away from all this food. I don't want him getting into it."

Anna went to the three mounds of food. Her first task was to separate the oats from the hay. Every once in awhile she looked up to check on Acorn and Rosalie. Rosalie was following Acorn all around the paddock. They were having a great time.

Anna wasn't having fun. It was hot in the shelter and the flies were as interested in Anna as Rosalie was interested in Acorn.

Suddenly, Rosalie came running up to

her. Acorn was close behind. That meant Anna would have to keep Acorn from getting into the piles of food — again. "I thought I asked you to keep Acorn away from the shelter," Anna said.

"He follows me everywhere," Rosalie said proudly. "I can't help it. And he wants to give me another ride."

"Oh no he doesn't," Anna said. "He wants to slow down and have a rest."

Acorn nosed around Anna and started munching some oats. "And keep him away from this mess," Anna shouted. "Haven't you caused enough trouble for one day?"

"I'm sorry," Rosalie said softly. "I thought you'd be glad I made the ponies dinner."

Rosalie turned and walked slowly across the paddock. Acorn followed her. Anna watched to be sure Rosalie closed the gate behind her. She didn't want Acorn to follow Rosalie home.

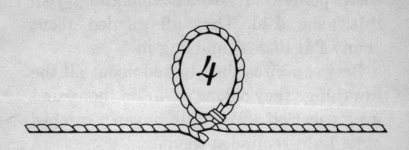

Anna's Great Idea

When Anna got to the Crandals', she let the twins help her unsaddle Acorn. Then she turned him out in the paddock with Lightning and Snow White.

Anna laughed when she saw the dinner that Pam and Lulu had prepared. They'd set out three individual pizzas on their favorite picnic rock near the paddock.

"We made them ourselves," Pam said.

Anna told Pam and Lulu about the three mounds of food Rosalie had prepared for their ponies. "It looked something like this," she said. They all giggled about "Pony Pal Pizzas" and dug in.

Between bites they talked about all the fun things they'd done so far on their summer vacation. "We still haven't camped out," Lulu reminded them.

"We sort of camp out when we have barn sleepovers," Anna said.

"I mean camping out in the wilderness," Lulu said. "With a tent."

"Would we take our ponies?" asked Pam.

"Absolutely," said Lulu. "And enough food for two days."

"Our parents would never let us," Anna said sadly.

"There has to be a way," said Lulu.

They all thought silently for a minute. Between them they knew they'd find a solution to this Pony Pal Problem.

"I've got it," Anna exclaimed. "We could camp out on the Wiggins estate. Our parents know Ms. Wiggins. And she'd know

where we were and everything."

"And our ponies would be rested in the morning," said Lulu. "So we could start from our campsite and go on Wiggins' trails we've never been on before."

Anna and Lulu were ready to hit high fives, but Pam wasn't. "We still have to ask our parents, *and* Ms. Wiggins," she said.

"Let's start with Ms. Wiggins," Anna suggested.

"My dad's having supper with her at the diner tonight," Lulu told the others.

"So let's go to the diner," said Pam.

Anna patted her pizza-filled stomach. "I'm starving," she said with a giggle.

When the three girls walked into Off-Main Diner, a voice called out, "Hey, look who's here." It was Lulu's father. They went over to the booth where he and Ms. Wiggins were eating blueberry pie with ice cream. "Order yourselves dessert on me," Mr. Sanders offered.

"Thanks," they all said together.

Ms. Wiggins told Lulu's dad how the girls and their ponies had visited Picasso and Winston earlier in the day. "Girls," she said, "there are interesting trails over on the west side of the estate. I'd love for you to ride on them sometime."

The Pony Pals exchanged a look. They couldn't believe it. It was as if Ms. Wiggins had read their minds.

"That's why we came looking for you," Lulu said.

"To ask you a favor," Pam put in.

"That has to do with those trails," Anna added.

The girls explained their idea of camping out on the Wiggins estate.

"Then our ponies will be fresh in the morning," Anna said, "and we can explore the trails to the west."

Ms. Wiggins smiled. "I know the perfect campsite for you," she said. "It's near a stream and not too far from my house.

There's a small corral that will be perfect for your ponies. And I have a tent I can set up for you."

Mr. Sanders said Lulu could camp out as long as the campsite was near Ms. Wiggins' mansion. Anna got her mother from the diner kitchen. After talking to Lulu's father and Ms. Wiggins, she agreed that Anna could go on the camping trip. Pam phoned her parents. They agreed that if Ms. Wiggins was involved, Pam could camp out, too.

"Now let's plan the trip and write everything down," Pam said.

The girls ordered brownies and milk and got paper and pencils from the kitchen. Then they went to their favorite booth to eat dessert and prepare for their camping trip.

"We can put our food and clothes in the saddlebags," Anna said.

"And move the sleeping bags to the back of the saddles," said Lulu.

Anna drew a pony outfitted with gear for a camping trip. Pam labeled the drawing.

Rain gear

Halter

Saddle bags

Sleeping bag

Lead rope

"Next we should plan our menus," Lulu said. "Then we'll know what food we need to buy."

"This trip is going to be so much fun," said Anna.

The girls decided what they and their ponies would eat on the camping trip. Lulu wrote their menus down.

LUNCH — DAY ONE

For us:

peanut butter and jelly sandwiches

apples

boxed fruit juices

For ponies:

water

grass

SNACK — DAY ONE

For us:

trail mix

water

For ponies:

water

apples

The girls were planning SUPPER — DAY ONE when they heard a familiar voice yelling, "That's them, Mom. The girls with the ponies!"

Oh, no, Anna thought, as she looked up to see Rosalie and her mother at the counter. Her mother's hair was blonde and

30

straight, just like Rosalie's. Rosalie came over to the Pony Pal booth. "Where's Acorn?" she asked.

Anna explained that Acorn and Snow White were having a sleepover with Lightning.

Rosalie looked at the papers spread out over the table. "How come you're doing homework?" she asked. "It's vacation."

"We're going on a camping trip," Lulu explained. "We have to make lists so we don't forget anything."

"We're real busy right now," Pam added.

"Rosalie," her mother called sharply. "Come get this ice-cream cone before it melts all over me."

"Coming," Rosalie answered. "See you tomorrow," she told the Pony Pals.

"Those are my new friends," they all heard Rosalie tell her mother.

Anna sighed and went back to working on the lists. At least Rosalie wouldn't be going on their camping trip.

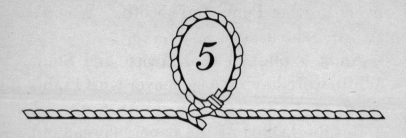

Beware of Rattlesnakes

The next morning the Pony Pals woke up from their sleepover in the barn. They fed their ponies and talked about the camping trip. They were still talking about their trip while eating breakfast in the Crandal kitchen. "I can't believe we're finally going *camping*!" Anna exclaimed.

After breakfast the girls saddled up their ponies and rode onto Pony Pal Trail. But they weren't going on a long trail ride. They were going straight to the Harley paddock.

The girls wanted their three ponies rested for the big camping trip the next day. Besides they had to shop for groceries and supplies.

They were in the fruit and vegetable section of the Green Market when Anna saw Rosalie's mother. She was weighing grapes for a customer.

"Look," Anna said to her friends, "that's Rosalie's mother."

They brought their bag of apples over to the woman.

"Hi," Anna said.

"Hi," Mrs. Lacey said back. "You're the girls with the horses." She didn't smile when she said it so Anna couldn't tell if she was being friendly or not. "Rosalie won't stop talking about horses," she said. "Day and night that's all I hear."

"I know," Anna said. "She really loves them."

Rosalie's mother sighed as she weighed the apples. "Why can't Rosalie like goldfish?" she asked no one in particular. "Goldfish I could handle. Or even a gerbil." She marked the price of the apples on the bag and handed it to Anna. "Don't encourage her, okay?" she said. "Because there's no way on earth that girl is ever going to have a horse. I have enough trouble paying the rent and buying food and clothes for her and her brother."

"We don't encourage her," Anna told Mrs. Lacey.

Another customer handed Mrs. Lacey a bunch of bananas to be weighed.

" 'Bye, Mrs. Lacey," Pam said.

"Yeah. 'Bye. You all have a nice day," she said. "You and those horses."

Anna didn't bother to tell her that their horses were ponies. And that ponies were smaller than horses. She knew Mrs. Lacey wouldn't care.

The Pony Pals were climbing the back stairs to Anna's house when Anna noticed Rosalie's blonde head bobbing around the paddock. Rosalie was back — again. When

she spotted the Pony Pals, Rosalie ran across the paddock toward the house. The three ponies trotted in a row behind her.

"She's like the Pied Piper of ponies," Lulu giggled.

The three ponies stopped at the fence and watched Rosalie hop over the top. Rosalie ran past the vegetable garden and up the stairs. Anna noticed she had a periwinkle-blue ribbon in her hair. The Pony Pal color!

"Rosalie, does your mother know where you are?" Anna asked.

"My brother does," she answered. "He takes care of me after day camp. He's thirteen. I told him I'm helping you get ready for your camping trip. He said you should watch out for rattlesnakes. He said rattlesnakes like dark, warm places — like sleeping bags."

"Is your brother Mike Lacey?" Pam asked.

"Uh-huh," Rosalie answered. "That's him."

The Pony Pals exchanged a look. They all knew Mike Lacey. He was best friends with the meanest, most annoying boy in the eighth grade — Tommy Rand. Mike Lacey was the *second* meanest, most annoying boy in the eighth grade.

"Tell your brother thanks for the advice," Lulu said. "And tell him we're not afraid of snakes. I camped a lot with my dad in places that had lots of snakes. Even poisonous ones."

"Maybe your brother's the one who's afraid of snakes," Pam added.

Anna thought, Rosalie has a mother who doesn't like horses and a pain for a brother. What about her father?

"Does your dad live with you?" she asked Rosalie.

"Not anymore," Rosalie said. "He lives in Ohio."

For the first time Anna felt sorry for Rosalie. But not for long.

"Can I ride Acorn?" Rosalie asked.

"Not today," Anna answered. "The ponies are resting for the trip."

"Can I have a ride when you come back from the trip?" she asked.

"I suppose," Anna answered.

"Can I have two rides because you'll be gone two days? Please say yes."

"We'll see," Anna answered.

Acorn neighed and Rosalie ran back to the paddock yelling, "Two rides on Acorn. Yippee!"

The next morning the Pony Pals met in the Harley paddock. Anna tied her sleeping bag to the back of her saddle. "This is going to be great," she said. Anna noticed that Rosalie was running across the paddock toward them. Anna was so happy about the camping trip that even Rosalie couldn't spoil her good mood. "Hi, Rosalie," she said cheerfully.

Rosalie didn't seem to hear her. She was hugging Acorn. "I came to say good-bye,

Acorn," she told the pony. "Have fun and come back safe."

Just then Lulu's father came out to the paddock. "Here's a little something for your trip," he said. He handed each of the campers a red plastic whistle. "Use these if you get separated. Or to signal if you need help."

Mrs. Harley was coming across the paddock carrying a package. Anna thought it looked about the size of three big brownies. But the package wasn't brownies. It was a first-aid kit. "I made this up for you," her mother explained. "There's antiseptic, Band-Aids, and an Ace bandage." Anna put the first-aid kit in her saddlebag next to her flashlight.

Grandmother Sanders came out, too. "I just heard on the radio that it is going to be very cold tonight," she said. "Maybe you should wait for better weather."

"We'll be okay, Grandma," Lulu said. She gave her grandmother a hug.

"Can I walk partway with you?" Rosalie asked Anna.

"It's time for you to go to day camp," Anna told her. "We're only going to be gone for two days."

"Oh, all right," Rosalie said. " 'Bye." She gave Acorn one last hug.

S.O.S.

At first the girls were riding on familiar trails. "So far it's just like a normal day of trail riding," Pam said.

Once they got to the Wiggins' mansion, Anna took out the map Ms. Wiggins had made for them. She checked the map and pointed with her riding crop to a wooded area on the right. "The campsite is this direction," she said. "There's the trail."

Anna and Acorn led the way. The campsite was an open area with dry leaves and pine needles. A gray, dome-shaped tent was set up on one side of the clearing. On the other side there was a small pony corral closed in by an old wood fence. Through the trees Anna saw the clear sparkling water of a stream.

"Sh-hh," Lulu said. "Listen." Even the ponies stayed perfectly still while they all listened to the gurgling of the stream and the chirping of a lone bird.

"It's perfect," Pam whispered.

The girls dismounted their ponies. Then they undid their sleeping bags and saddle-bags and put them on the ground. Next they removed their ponies' tack. They left on bridles and halters so they could lead the ponies to the stream for water and grass.

After they put the ponies in their corral, Anna shouted, "Race you!" The Pony Pals ran across the clearing to the tent.

They all got there at the same time, but took turns crawling through the flap opening.

"It's bigger inside than it looks from the outside," Pam said.

"And look," Anna said, "Ms. Wiggins left us stuff."

In the middle of the tent floor there was a red bucket, a plastic gallon jug of water, and a note.

Pam opened the note. The others looked over her shoulder as she read it aloud.

Dear Campers :

I will come by for dinner. We'll make a campfire. Have a great afternoon trail riding.

Love,
W.

P.S. The bucket is so your ponies can have stream water in the corral tonight. The bottled water is for you.

The girls ate lunch in front of their tent. After lunch Lulu strung their food up in a tree so animals wouldn't get it. Then they put the rest of their supplies in the tent.

Even though Anna didn't believe anything Mike Lacey said about snakes, she decided to leave her sleeping bag rolled up until she went to bed. She noticed that Pam and Lulu did the same thing.

Acorn nuzzled Anna happily when she tacked him up for an afternoon ride. "We're going places we've never been before," she told him. "And then we're coming back here for the night. It'll be very dark and fun." She gave her pony a hug. It was great to have Acorn all to herself again.

The Pony Pals followed the map Ms. Wiggins had made for them of the western section of the Wiggins estate. It was as beautiful and interesting as Ms. Wiggins had promised. They found a pond with a turtle as big as a dinner plate. And when Pam was in the lead position, she saw a fox run across their path.

At the top of a particularly steep hill, they walked their ponies over to the edge of the trail to look at the view. "This is the highest we've ever climbed," said Anna.

"Oh, look!" Lulu said. She pointed to a large hawk gliding on a wind current.

"There's Mount Morris," Pam said, pointing to the east.

"Someday we'll camp over there," said Lulu.

They were going down the steep hill when they heard a high-pitched sound. "Was that a bird?" Pam asked.

They heard the noise again. This time there was one short blast followed by a long one and another short one. "That's the S.O.S. signal my father and I use," Lulu said.

"Someone's in trouble," Anna said.

"Or is trying to find us," Lulu said. "Someone who knows the signal."

Lulu took out her whistle and blew one long whistle. "That's what we do to let the other person know we heard them," she explained.

A long whistle answered Lulu's signal. This time the girls noticed that it came from the direction they'd come from.

"Let's go," Lulu said. "Whoever needs us is coming this way."

"You take the lead," Pam told Anna. "Acorn's best on this rocky terrain. He gives our ponies confidence."

As they went down the steep incline, Anna felt proud of Acorn. But she was also feeling afraid. Who was sending them an S.O.S. signal? And why?

When they reached the foot of the hill, Pam blew her whistle. This time the answering whistle was even closer.

A few minutes later Anna saw Picasso and Ms. Wiggins coming around a bend in the trail. Anna turned in the saddle and told the others, "It's just Ms. Wiggins."

Anna figured Ms. Wiggins was looking for them just to be sure they were okay. But when Ms. Wiggins got closer, Anna saw a grim look on her face. Something was terribly wrong.

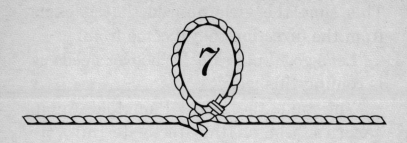

Emergency!

The Pony Pals pulled their ponies up in front of Ms. Wiggins and Picasso.

"What's wrong?" Anna asked.

"Rosalie is missing," Ms. Wiggins answered. "Lulu's father called to tell me. We decided I should find you girls. You might be able to help."

"What could have happened to her?" asked Anna.

"We just saw Rosalie this morning," said Lulu.

"Did someone kidnap her?" asked Pam.

"Let's go back to your campsite," Ms. Wiggins said, "and I'll tell you everything I know."

The three girls and Ms. Wiggins rode in silence. They were all concentrating on keeping up a good pace. And worrying about Rosalie.

While the ponies and Picasso drank from the stream and munched on grass, Ms. Wiggins told the girls what she knew.

"Mike Lacey went to pick up his sister at day camp," she began. "They told him that she hadn't been there all day. He went over to your house, Anna, to see if Rosalie was there. Your mother told him that Rosalie had been by in the morning. And that she said she was going to day camp.

"Next," Ms. Wiggins continued, "Mike went to the Green Market to tell his mother Rosalie was missing. They both checked their apartment to make sure Rosalie hadn't gone home while Mike was looking for her. Then they phoned their friends and neighbors in town. It seems no one has seen

Rosalie since nine o'clock this morning. Mrs. Lacey notified the state police. Everyone is looking for Rosalie. As of an hour ago she hadn't been found."

Pam looked at her watch. "It's five o'clock now. Rosalie's been missing for eight hours."

They were all silent for a few seconds as they thought about what a long time eight hours could be. Anna was trying to figure out where Rosalie went. Had she cut day camp and just forgotten about the time? Or had she wandered off by herself and gotten lost?

Anna looked over and saw that Acorn was watching her. Anna thought he had a sad look in his eyes.

Ms. Wiggins broke the silence. "Mrs. Lacey said Rosalie spent a lot of time with you three over the last few days."

"She kept hanging around us," Anna told Ms. Wiggins. "It started with the pony rides at the firehouse fair."

"She can be a pain," Lulu said. "But we

were nice enough to her. Especially Anna."

Anna wasn't sure she'd been "nice enough" to Rosalie.

"Do you have any idea where Rosalie might have gone?" Ms. Wiggins asked.

The three girls looked at one another and nodded. They all had the same idea.

"Maybe she tried to follow us," Anna said. "She's always wanting to do whatever we do."

Pam and Lulu said they agreed with Anna.

"Maybe we should form our own search party," Lulu said to Ms. Wiggins.

"We could start here and go back over the trails we took this morning," suggested Pam.

"And we should ride our ponies when we're looking for her," said Anna. "That way we can move fast and give Rosalie a ride if we find her. Acorn likes Rosalie and I think he'd want to help."

Ms. Wiggins agreed that the girls should look for Rosalie. Meanwhile, she told them, she'd ride Picasso back to her place to phone the Town Hall. "That's where they've set up headquarters for the search party," she explained. "I'll tell them you think Rosalie might have followed you. I can fax them a map of the trails. Then they can start *their* search from where you started out this morning."

Ms. Wiggins put the bridle on Picasso. "I'll meet up with you on the trail," she said. "If Rosalie's already been found I'll signal by one short and one long blast of my whistle while I'm riding."

"And if we find her we'll do the same," Lulu said. "That way you can let everybody know."

"If you find Rosalie in bad shape, or you need help yourselves, don't forget to send out the S.O.S. signal," Ms. Wiggins said.

"Maybe you should tell the search party the signals we're using," Lulu told Ms. Wiggins.

"Good idea," she said. Ms. Wiggins

mounted Picasso, wished the Pony Pals good luck, and rode off.

Anna looked up at the sky. The blue sky of a few minutes before had turned gray with storm clouds, and the temperature had dropped.

Anna shivered.

"All Rosalie had on this morning was shorts and a T-shirt," Lulu said.

If Rosalie was in the woods, Anna thought, would they be able to find her by nightfall? Or would the six-year-old girl be spending the night alone in the woods without shelter, warm clothes, food, or water?

8

The Clue in Badd Brook

The Pony Pals got ready for the big search. Anna put her extra sweater in her saddlebag next to the first-aid kit and flashlight. She refilled her water bottle and put that in the other saddlebag with her trail mix.

Lulu got the idea to hang their whistles around their necks. They used the rawhide shoestrings they'd brought for emergency bridle repairs.

The girls worked quickly and efficiently. This wasn't playing. This wasn't a game.

They had an important job to do. Rosalie's safety was at stake. Maybe even her life.

As the Pony Pals put the bridles on their ponies and tightened the saddle girths, they talked about how they would conduct the search.

Lulu knew a lot about tracking animals and people from her many camping trips with her father.

"We're looking for signs that she's been on the trail — or where she might have gone off it," Lulu told Pam and Anna. "So keep an eye out for footprints, broken branches, or pieces of torn clothing."

"What colors was she wearing this morning?" Pam asked.

"She had on a yellow T-shirt," Lulu remembered. "And red shorts."

"And that periwinkle-blue ribbon in her hair," Anna said. "Like the ones we used in our ponies' manes for the firehouse fair."

As they mounted their ponies, Pam said she'd look for clues on the left-hand side of

the trail. Lulu said she'd look on the right. Anna, who took the lead, would watch for clues straight ahead.

They rode in silence so they could concentrate on searching for clues and listening for any sign of Rosalie. But every five minutes or so the Pony Pals purposely made a lot of noise. They hollered out "Rosalie." Then they halted their ponies and listened carefully to hear if Rosalie answered.

"Look how good our ponies are about all the noise we're making," Lulu commented to the others.

"I think they know we're doing something important," Anna said. She leaned over and patted Acorn's neck. "You're going to help us find Rosalie, aren't you, Acorn?" Acorn nickered in response.

As the search continued, Anna wondered how Rosalie felt. Anna knew that if *she* were lost in those woods when she was only six years old, she'd be *terrified*. Anna decided that Rosalie would be thinking all sorts of horrible things — like never being found and starving to death. Maybe she would imagine swarms of killer bees or millions of biting red ants or attacking wolves. And Rosalie definitely would be remembering what her brother said about rattlesnakes.

Soon the Pony Pals came to the wide section of Badd Brook that they'd crossed in the morning. Fast-moving water rushed over boulders and rocks.

"She couldn't cross this without a horse," Lulu said.

"But what if she *tried* to cross it," Anna wondered out loud. "Then fell and got dragged by the water."

"Let's walk along the edge of the brook," Lulu suggested, "toward the waterfall."

This was the first time any of them mentioned the waterfall. And that's all that was said. The thought of Rosalie being swept over the waterfall was too scary to say out loud.

While Acorn stepped carefully along the

uneven bank of the brook, Anna kept a sharp eye out for clues. Suddenly, she noticed something bright blue in the water. She halted Acorn and dismounted.

"Why'd you stop?" Pam asked as she halted behind Anna.

Anna slipped Acorn's reins over his head and handed them to Pam. "Hold him," she said. Then Anna jumped on three rocks to get closer to the flash of blue color in the water. Planting both her feet on the third rock, she squatted and put her hand in the cold stream. She pulled out a ribbon that had been caught on the sharp edge of a mossy rock. Anna jumped the rocks back to solid ground. She held up a periwinkle-blue ribbon for the others to see.

Without saying a word, the other two yelled "Rosalie." They waited and listened carefully. The only answer they heard was the sound of the brook rushing toward the waterfall.

The Pony Pals were on foot leading their ponies toward the waterfall when Acorn suddenly stopped in his tracks. "He doesn't want to go this way," Anna told Pam and Lulu.

"Maybe he's afraid of the sound of the waterfall," said Lulu.

"He's never cared about that before," Anna said.

"Maybe he got a pebble in his hoof," suggested Pam. "If you need the hoof pick, I've got it in my saddlebag."

Anna checked Acorn's hooves. No pebbles. But Acorn still wouldn't go forward.

"What is it, Acorn?" Anna asked her pony. "What's wrong?"

In the Deer Run

Acorn neighed and lowered his head. What if he has colic? Anna thought. She knew that horses could die from colic. But Acorn didn't seem sick. He was just sniffing the ground and pawing at a mess of deer hoofprints in the mud.

Anna bent over and looked more carefully at the ground herself. There, among the deer hoofprints, she saw the clue they'd been looking for. The imprint of a small sneaker.

"Look!" Anna pointed to the ground. Pam and Lulu walked over.

"It has to be Rosalie's," Lulu concluded. "No other kids would have been around here today."

"That means she made it across the brook," said Pam.

"And didn't get dragged over the waterfall," Lulu added.

Anna patted Acorn's neck. "Good detective work, Acorn," she said.

"But where's Rosalie now?" Lulu wondered out loud.

They looked for more of Rosalie's footprints. But there was just that one.

Anna looked at how the deer prints led into the underbrush. The only way to walk through it was on a narrow path that the white-tailed deer made. "This run isn't wide enough or high enough for a riding trail," Anna told her friends. "But Rosalie wouldn't know that."

"And she probably doesn't know the difference between a deer's hoofprint and a horse's hoofprint," said Lulu. "She must have thought our ponies made these marks."

"I'll bet she went into the woods this way," Anna concluded. "I'll go through the deer run and look for her."

The girls decided that since Lulu knew the most about tracking, she should go with Anna and Acorn. And that Pam would stay behind with Snow White and Lightning to wait for Ms. Wiggins.

"Don't go too far," Pam warned. "And use your whistles if you need help."

The two girls and the pony entered the narrow, dark path.

"Rosalie," Anna called out. "Acorn is here to give you a ride. Where are you?"

"Rosalie," Lulu yelled. "If you hear us, shout back."

They stopped and listened. But all they heard was an owl's *who who-oo*.

The two girls and the pony came to a fork in the deer run. "Which way should we go?" Lulu asked.

Acorn snorted and pulled to his right. "Acorn thinks we should go this way," Anna told Lulu.

The girls took Acorn's advice and turned right. They walked slowly along the deer run looking for clues and calling for Rosalie.

Acorn pulled on the rein again. He wanted to move faster. Anna let him set the pace and the two girls kept up with him.

Acorn stopped abruptly. Had he found Rosalie? Anna looked at the tangled undergrowth to her right. No Rosalie. She looked to her left. No Rosalie. She looked straight ahead. A small figure in red shorts and a yellow T-shirt was coming around a turn in the path. Rosalie saw the two girls and Acorn at the same instant they saw her. She ran toward them.

Anna squatted and opened her arms to Rosalie. But Rosalie ran right past Anna and threw her arms around Acorn. "Oh, Acorn," she said in a hoarse whisper, "you found me."

Lulu and Anna smiled at each other. Then they raised their whistles to their lips and blew one short and one long blast.

Anna could see that Rosalie was scratched up and shivering with the cold. And she was speaking to Acorn in the raspy voice of someone whose voice is all worn out from shouting.

"Are you all right?" Lulu asked Rosalie.

Rosalie straightened herself up and said, "I'm okay. I went for a walk." She looked around the woods. "It's pretty in the woods."

Anna took her sweater out of the saddlebag and wrapped it around Rosalie's shivering shoulders. "I forgot my sweater," Rosalie whispered. "Thanks."

Anna and Lulu exchanged a glance. They both knew that when you rescue someone you have to be sure they aren't suffering from serious injuries or shock before you move them.

Anna sat on the pine-needle-covered path. "Sit down and we'll rest for a minute," she told Rosalie.

Rosalie sat down next to Anna. "I'm not tired," she said.

"It's six o'clock at night," Lulu said. "You've been walking in the woods all day. Your mother's been very worried about you. We've all been worried."

"Well, maybe I got a *little* lost," Rosalie said. Tears gathered in her eyes. She gulped to keep from crying. "But I wasn't scared."

Anna handed Rosalie her water bottle. "Don't drink it too fast," she cautioned.

While Rosalie drank the water and ate some trail mix, Anna carefully cleaned off her scratches with the antiseptic from the first-aid kit.

They all heard the *whacka whacka whacka* of a helicopter overhead. They looked up but couldn't see it through the cover of trees.

"I'll bet that's the state police," Lulu told Rosalie. "Looking for you."

"Is *everyone* looking for me?" Rosalie asked.

"*Everyone*," Anna and Lulu both answered.

Rosalie opened her hand and Acorn bent over for a nibble of trail mix. "But Acorn's the one who found me," Rosalie said.

"Yeah," Anna told Rosalie. "Acorn found you. But don't give him any more trail mix, okay?"

"Okay," Rosalie said.

"But you could give him some water in your hand," Anna suggested.

"Okay," Rosalie said. She poured some water in her hand and held it out for the pony to lick.

"How would you like to ride out of the woods on Acorn?" Anna asked.

"Will it count as one of my two rides for when you get back from your camping trip?"

"No," Anna answered with a smile. "I'll still owe you two rides."

No More Ponies

Anna put her riding helmet on Rosalie and helped her mount Acorn. Then Anna took the reins and led her pony and his passenger along the deer run. "You might have to duck for some branches," Anna warned her. Rosalie leaned forward in the saddle, wrapped her arms loosely around Acorn's neck . . . and fell fast asleep.

Lulu walked on the other side of Acorn to be sure Rosalie didn't slip off the pony. But both Lulu and Anna could see how

careful Acorn was being with his special passenger.

When they came out at Badd Brook, Ms. Wiggins and Picasso were there waiting with Pam and the two ponies. Ms. Wiggins looked alarmed when she saw Rosalie slumped over Acorn. "What's happened to her?" she asked.

Anna smiled at Ms. Wiggins. "Rosalie's okay. She's just tired."

The Pony Pals and Ms. Wiggins led their horses along the trail back to the mansion. Ms. Wiggins said she'd heard their whistle blasts signaling that Rosalie had been found and was okay. "So I rode home and called town," she said. "Mrs. Lacey should know by now that her daughter is safe. She'll be very grateful to you girls for rescuing Rosalie."

Then the girls told Ms. Wiggins about the clues they'd put together to find Rosalie.

"You're real heros," Ms. Wiggins said. "The whole town should be proud of you."

"Acorn's a hero, too," Anna said.

The first thing Anna noticed as they approached the Wiggins mansion was that the town ambulance and a state trooper car were parked out front. The second thing she noticed was Mrs. Lacey running in their direction. The third thing she noticed was that Mike Lacey and Tommy Rand were right behind Mrs. Lacey.

Rosalie was awake now and sitting tall in the saddle. She waved to her mother. Mrs. Lacey called out, "Oh my baby. Oh my Rosalie." When she reached them, Mrs. Lacey told Ms. Wiggins, "Get my child off that animal." Anna heard anger in Mrs. Lacey's voice.

Ms. Wiggins helped Rosalie dismount Acorn and took off the riding helmet. Mrs. Lacey wrapped her little girl in her arms and hugged and kissed her. "Are you okay?" the tearful mother asked over and over.

During this mother-daughter reunion,

Mike Lacey and Tommy Rand came up to the Pony Pals. "You lost my sister," Mike accused. "You could have killed her."

"What do you expect from the Pony Pests?" Tommy Rand hissed.

Pam, Lulu, and Anna knew that they should just ignore them, but they couldn't ignore Mrs. Lacey.

"It's your fault that Rosalie got lost," Mrs. Lacey said to the Pony Pals. "You encouraged her to follow you. Why don't you play with kids your own age? You and those horses. You just leave my child alone."

"But Acorn *saved* me," Rosalie told her mother. "He *found* me."

"Hush," Mrs. Lacey told Rosalie. She put an arm around her daughter and pulled her close.

Ms. Wiggins tried to explain what really happened, but she was interrupted by the ambulance pulling up next to them. A medic hopped out of the front seat and two emergency medical team vounteers came out the back doors.

"Do I have to go the hospital, Mom?" Rosalie asked. "I'm not sick."

"We can start by checking her over here, ma'am," the medic told Mrs. Lacey.

The medic squatted in front of Rosalie. "You've had quite an adventure, young lady," he said. "I'll bet you're plenty thirsty."

Rosalie pointed to the Pony Pals. "They gave me lots of water," she said. "But I had to drink it slow. Acorn's the one who found me."

The medic opened his black medical bag. "I see some scratches that should be cleaned up here," he said.

"They already cleaned them," Rosalie told him.

The medic took a closer look at the scratches on Rosalie's arms and legs. Then he looked over at the Pony Pals. "Good work," he said. The Pony Pals smiled at each other. At least *somebody* appreciated them.

A few minutes later the medic said Rosalie was okay. "You can bring her right home," he told her mother. "But I'd keep her there for a day or two. Be sure she rests and takes plenty of fluids."

As the ambulance pulled away, Mrs. Lacey told Mike, "You'll have to stay with her tomorrow. I've got to work."

"But, Ma, I have a baseball game," he said.

Mrs. Lacey put her hands on her hips. "You will do what I say, Michael Lacey," she said. "Now get back in the police car. He said he'd bring us home."

Anna saw Mike mimic Mrs. Lacey behind her back. But he did what she said.

"Mom, I *can't* stay home," Rosalie informed her mother. "I've got *two* rides on Acorn to take. Two. I want one tomorrow."

Mrs. Lacey glared at the Pony Pals. "You promised her more rides?" Then she turned to Rosalie. "No pony rides. No more ponies. You are not to go near those girls. Or their horses. Do you understand?"

She grabbed Rosalie's hand, turned, and walked away. But not before Anna noticed that for the first time since she'd been found, Rosalie Lacey was crying.

A Letter for Acorn

Ms. Wiggins and the Pony Pals watched Mrs. Lacey and Rosalie get in the police car.

"I can't believe she's blaming us that Rosalie ran away and got lost," Lulu said.

"All we did was try to help," Pam said.

"She's being unfair," Anna added.

"I know," Ms. Wiggins said. "But Mrs. Lacey's too upset to listen to anyone right now. She's been through a lot."

"I just want to go back to our campsite," Anna told Pam and Lulu.

Ms. Wiggins looked to the west where the sun was dropping behind a ridge. "It'll be getting dark soon," she said. "You should hurry. I'll come along in a few minutes with the hot dogs and corn. We'll make a great campfire."

The Pony Pals and Ms. Wiggins had a delicious, fun-filled supper around the campfire. They cooked hot dogs on sticks. They roasted corn in the husks. For dessert they made sandwiches of toasted marsh-mallows and chocolate bars between graham crackers.

Ms. Wiggins said that the Pony Pals should be proud of what they did. If it hadn't been for them, Rosalie could still be lost.

"It's so dark tonight," Lulu said.

"And cold," said Pam as she drew closer to the warmth of the campfire.

After Ms. Wiggins and Picasso left, the three girls went to their tent.

Later, feeling cozy in her warm sleeping

bag, Anna looked up at the stars through the tent netting. She was happy that the Pony Pals were finally camping out. And she was happy that they'd found Rosalie and that she was okay.

Anna just wished she hadn't seen Rosalie cry. There must be something the Pony Pals could do to help her.

The next morning Anna was the first of the Pony Pals to wake up. She pulled the tent flap open and stuck her head out. A nighttime chill was still in the air and the ground was wet with dew. She saw that all three ponies were asleep standing up in the corral.

Anna lay there watching the ponies wake up and the morning brightening. Through the trees she saw three white-tailed deer drinking from the stream. And she watched a squirrel run up and down a tree with nuts to put away for winter. She even saw a garter snake slithering through the ground cover of dead leaves and pine needles.

Now Lulu and Pam woke up and the three girls fed the ponies and ate breakfast. The ponies had oats and grass. The girls had peanut butter and jelly sandwiches and orange juice.

The Pony Pals spent the morning following Ms. Wiggins' map of trail rides to the west. At noon they returned to the campsite to eat lunch and to pack up their equipment. Then they trail-rode home.

By four o'clock the three best friends and their ponies had reached Pony Pal Trail. It was time to say good-bye to Pam and Lightning.

"I guess our camping trip is officially over," Anna said.

They all agreed that their camping trip was one of the best Pony Pal times ever.

"But Rosalie being lost was scary," said Pam. "I'm really glad she wasn't injured or something."

They all agreed about that, too.

"I wonder if Rosalie will ever get a chance to ride again?" Lulu asked.

"Not until she doesn't live with her mother anymore," Anna said.

"I wish we could help her," said Pam.

"Me, too," Lulu added. "Maybe we should try to talk to her mother."

"Mrs. Lacey hates us," Anna said. "Especially me."

"This sounds like a Pony Pal Problem," said Pam.

"We need a plan," said Lulu. "Let's all think of what we can do so Rosalie can be with ponies again."

"We'll use our Pony Pal Power," Pam said.

"It'd be great if we could help Rosalie," said Anna.

Anna and Lulu said good-bye to Pam. As Anna rode home she thought of how sad she'd be if she couldn't be around ponies.

Lulu and Anna were bringing their ponies' bridles and saddles into the shelter when something caught Anna's eye. It was a plastic bag on top of the feed box. As she got closer, she saw two carrots and two ap-

ples in the bag. Under the bag was a folded
piece of paper.

"It's a note or something," Lulu said.

Anna put down the tack she was carrying
and picked up the note. She and Lulu read
it together.

ACORN THANK YOU
I ♡ YOU
ROSALIE

"Poor Rosalie," Anna said. "Lulu, we've
got to do something."

Three Ideas

The next morning the Pony Pals met in the Harley paddock to discuss what to do about Rosalie Lacey.

Pam showed Anna and Lulu her idea.

Rosalie should play with Jack and Jill instead of us.

"I talked to the twins about Rosalie," Pam said. "They know her from school.

She's a year older than they are, but they like her."

"If Rosalie played with Jack and Jill, she'd get to be around horses a lot," Lulu said.

"My mother knows Rosalie's mom from Parents Association at school," Pam said. "And my mother is going to Green Market this morning. To shop . . . and to invite Rosalie to play at our house."

"Great!" Anna said.

"Listen to my idea," Lulu said. She read:

We should talk to Mrs. Lacey.
No matter how mean she acts.

"We've got to get her to understand it wasn't our fault Rosalie ran away," Lulu said.

"But we shouldn't talk to her until *after* my mother's talked to her," Pam said.

"And no matter how Mrs. Lacey acts, we stick it out," Lulu said. "Right, Anna?"

Even though she was feeling angry and a little scared about talking to Mrs. Lacey, Anna agreed.

"What's *your* idea, Anna?" Lulu asked.

Anna showed her friends her idea.

Anna explained that her idea was to get Mrs. Lacey to let Rosalie ride Acorn again.

They all thought that Mrs. Lacey would probably let Rosalie play with the twins. Maybe she'd finally understand that it wasn't the Pony Pals' fault that Rosalie ran away. But how would they ever convince Mrs. Lacey to let Rosalie ride horses?

Around ten-thirty the three girls walked into the fruit and vegetable section of Green Market. Mrs. Lacey was unloading potatoes from a cloth sack into a bin. When she looked up and saw the Pony Pals, she frowned.

"Uh-oh," Anna groaned.

Mrs. Lacey finished dumping the potatoes and walked over to them. Anna was sure she was going to yell. She wanted to turn around and leave, but Lulu grabbed her arm.

Mrs. Lacey was still frowning when she told Pam that Rosalie was playing with the Crandal twins on Saturday. Anna couldn't figure out if Mrs. Lacey was angry at them or just nervous and shy.

"How is Rosalie feeling?" Pam asked her.

"She went back to day camp today," Mrs. Lacey said. She shifted uneasily from one foot to the other. "I want to thank you girls for finding Rosalie. I blamed you for her getting lost. But I know now that it was Mike's fault. He was supposed to bring her to day camp. Instead, he'd been letting her go alone."

The Pony Pals exchanged a glance. Mike's fault, not theirs. Anna could barely keep from smiling over that.

"The *County Times* called to ask me about Rosalie being lost," Mrs. Lacey said. "There's going to be an article saying you found her. You and your horses."

"Thank you," Lulu said.

"I'm glad you don't blame us anymore," said Pam.

"Rosalie's a nice kid," Anna said. "She's very smart and she's good with ponies."

"I guess just because I never liked horses doesn't mean Rosalie can't," Mrs. Lacey said. She finally smiled. Anna knew for sure that she'd just been nervous before. And maybe a little embarrassed about how she'd yelled at them the night of the rescue.

"Anyway, thanks again," Mrs. Lacey said. "Now I've got to get back to work."

When the Pony Pals were outside the store, Pam and Lulu raised their hands for high fives. But Anna held back.

"I forgot to do my idea," she said. "Wait here."

Anna ran back into the store. In a minute she came back out with a big smile on her face and told her friends. "She said yes! — Rosalie can ride."

The Pony Pals hit high fives and cheered, *"All right!"*

The next day was Saturday. At nine o'clock Mike brought Rosalie to the paddock, just as Anna had planned with Mrs. Lacey.

Acorn ran across the paddock to greet Rosalie. She gave him a big hug.

"Hi, Pony Pest," Mike said to Anna.

Rosalie glared at her brother. "Hey, quit

talking to my friend like that," she said, "or I'll tell Mom."

"Don't listen to him, Rosalie," Anna said.

"Pony Pals!" Mike said. "It's all so *stupid.*"

He turned and left the paddock. "Don't forget to pick me up at four o'clock," Rosalie called after him. "And don't be late."

When Mike was gone, Rosalie and Anna smiled at one another. "I like ponies better than boys," Rosalie said.

"Me, too," Anna said.

"I'm going to play with Jack and Jill Crandal," Rosalie said. "They like ponies."

"They *love* ponies," Anna said.

"My mom said you'd give me a ride today," said Rosalie.

"That's right," Anna said. "And a ride every week until school starts. Today, how would you like to ride over to the Crandals' on Pony Pal Trail?"

"Ride on the trail? What about you?" Rosalie asked.

"I get to ride Acorn lots," Anna said. "While you're playing with the twins, Acorn and I are going trail riding with Pam and Lulu. So you can ride Acorn all the way there."

"Yippee!" Rosalie said.

Anna pushed her fingers through Acorn's thick, black mane. She loved seeing Rosalie so happy. Acorn nickered and nudged Anna's shoulder.

Anna gave her pony a big hug and a kiss.

Dear Reader:

I am having a lot of fun researching and writing books about the Pony Pals. I've met many interesting kids and adults who love ponies. And I've visited some wonderful ponies at homes, farms, and riding schools.

Before writing Pony Pals I wrote fourteen novels for children and young adults. Four of these were honored by Children's Choice Awards.

I live in Sharon, Connecticut, with my husband, Lee, and our dog, Willie. Our daughter is all grown up and has her own apartment in New York City.

Besides writing novels I like to draw, paint, garden, and swim. I didn't have a pony when I was growing up, but I have always loved them and dreamt about riding. Now I take riding lessons on a horse named Saz.

I like reading and writing about ponies as much as I do riding. Which proves to me that you don't have to ride a pony to love them. And you certainly don't need a pony to be a Pony Pal.

Happy Reading,

Jeanne Betancourt